It Zwibble
and the Hunt for the Rain Forest Treasure

Created by
WereRoss and WerEnko

Written by Lisa V. Werenko

Illustrated by Tom Ross

SCHOLASTIC INC.

New York Toronto London Auckland Sydney

Dedicated to the little ones
who know treasure when they
find it

ISBN 0-590-44841-2
Copyright © 1992 by WereRoss & WerEnko
All rights reserved. Published by Scholastic Inc.

12 11 10 9 8 7 6 5 4 3 2 1   2 3 4 5 6 7/9

Printed in the U.S.A.   24

First Scholastic printing, April 1992

In the Buzzville forest at the Zwibble Dibble mill there lives a dinosaur fairy named It Zwibble, a lot of star-tailed dinosaur babies called the Zwibble Dibbles, and some funny forest animal friends. The Zwibble family spend most of their days taking care of the planet earth.

BIRD SEED

For a very long time, the Zwibbles had been trying to find a way to save the lives of the many trees and animals in a special kind of forest far away from their Buzzville forest home, called the rain forest. Acres and acres of trees and plants were being chopped down. Many of the rain forest animals had no place to live.

It Zwibble had a plan to save the rain forest. He discovered that if the members of the Zwibble family saved their pennies, they could buy land in the rain forest. That way the Zwibble family could make sure that the animals living on *their* land would be safe!

Soon the whole family was taking part in the plan to save the rain forest. Everyone in the family chose a job to do.

Orbit's job was to go to the mailbox and pick up the mail. Every day his wheelbarrow was heavy with letters from children all over the world who wanted to help the Zwibbles save the rain forest.

Finally, Orbit had had enough! "Not one of these letters is for me!" he shouted. "I'm tired of working so hard for the earth!"

Orbit put the wheelbarrow down. He decided he would rather play his favorite game than work.

Orbit's favorite game was called Treasure Hunt. It Zwibble had taught him to play the game a long time ago. First Orbit put on his pirate hat. Then he'd call out "Finders keepers!" and head off in search of treasure.

Orbit was in the middle of searching for his latest treasure when It Zwibble came around the corner.

Orbit took a break from his treasure hunting to visit
with It Zwibble.

"I know how much you love to play Treasure Hunt," It Zwibble
told Orbit. "So do I! But the animals of the rain forest need our
help now."

"Why don't you just use your magic powers and save the
rain forest?" Orbit asked.

"Some things cannot be saved by magic alone," It Zwibble explained.

"Well, I don't care about that silly old rain forest," Orbit
grumbled. "It's not mine. I've never even seen it!"

It Zwibble showed Orbit pictures of beautiful rain forest plants and animals. "We get medicines from those leaves," It Zwibble explained. "The rain forest even cleans the air we breathe. I know you'd love it, Orbit. The rain forest is full of wonderful treasures!"

That night, Orbit stood in front of the window. He remembered how It Zwibble had said: "The rain forest is full of wonderful treasures."

"I'm gonna get some of that treasure for myself," Orbit said.

Orbit took a pinch of magic stardust from the Zwibble Dibble magical jar—just enough to help him fly to the rain forest. He sprinkled the magic dust all over himself. Then he called out "Finders keepers!" and flew off to the rain forest!

After a long time, Orbit landed under a beautiful canopy of leaves and flowers. The air was fresh and clean. "This must be the rain forest," Orbit thought. Then he heard the oddest sound. "Buuuurp–Booh-Hoo! Buuuuurp–Booh-Hoo!"

Up there in the trees sat a beautiful emerald green bird with feathers that slanted to the left. The beautiful bird was crying.

"They've cut down the trees where we made our homes," the bird sobbed. "I may be the only emerald slanty bird left in the world. If I don't find a mate and have a nest full of slanties, there won't be any slanty birds left on Earth."

"I'd like to help you," Orbit called up to the bird. "But I'm on a treasure hunt. See my hat?"

The bird grew silent. Orbit went off into the forest shouting "Finders keepers!"

Orbit was busy hunting treasure when he saw the leaves of the medicine plant. The leaves were so big and red.
"They look like rubies!" he exclaimed.

He stopped for a drink at a stream. The water was so clean and bright. "It glimmers like diamonds!" Orbit thought.

A beautiful family of leopards crossed Orbit's path.
They looked at Orbit. Their eyes shone like sapphires.

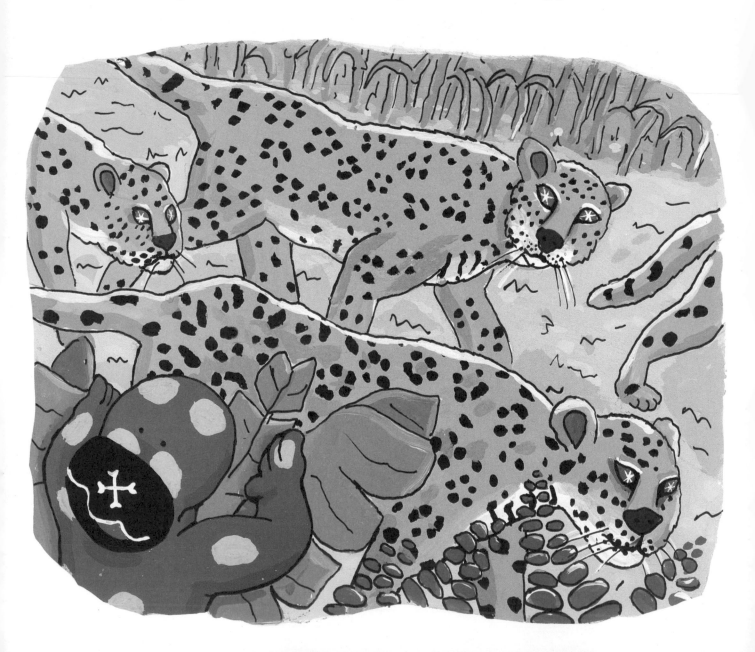

Orbit walked on searching for treasure. When he grew weary
he sat on a rock to rest. The sun was beginning to set.
The sunlight made the leaves of the trees shimmer like gold.
"It's beautiful here," Orbit whispered. "Just like It Zwibble said."

After his rest, Orbit continued on. He hadn't traveled very far when the forest area ended. There were no trees for miles and miles. All the trees and plants had been chopped down. "Oh no!" cried Orbit. "Where is the rain forest?"

It was dark and quiet. There were no animals to be seen.
They had all been chased away from their homes—just like
the emerald slanty bird.

Sadly, Orbit sat down on a log. The stars began to peek through the dark sky. Orbit looked up. The stars reminded him of home and his favorite star-touched dinosaur, It Zwibble. Then he remembered what It Zwibble had told him. You must never give up hope!

Orbit made a wish upon a star. He wished he could do something to save the rain forest and its creatures. The star shot across the sky in a blaze of light.

Suddenly the silence was broken by a strange sound.
"Buuuurp–Booh-Hoo! Buuurp–Booh-Hoo!"
   Orbit looked up and saw a beautiful bird with emerald
feathers that slanted to the right.
   "Why, you must be the mate to the other emerald slanty
bird!" Orbit shouted up to the bird. "Come with me, I'll help you
find your mate!"
   The bird followed Orbit back into the forest.

"Slanty bird! Slanty bird! Where are you?" Orbit cried out.
But no one answered.

Orbit and the bird searched for the other emerald slanty.
But they couldn't find her anywhere.

Suddenly, Orbit heard a rustling through the bushes. Out walked the beautiful emerald slanty's mate!

It was a very happy moment when left met right.

Orbit helped the slanty birds settle into a tree far from where the tree cutters could harm them. Then he said his good-byes. Orbit was going home.

"But what about your treasure hunt?" asked the birds.
    Orbit thought of the ruby-red leaves of the medicine plants, the sapphire eyes of the leopards, the stream water that shone like diamonds, and the magnificent emerald slanty birds.
    "I think I've found my treasure." Orbit smiled. "And now I want to go home and keep it safe."

And that's just what he did!

One day Orbit was sorting the mail when he found a postcard addressed just to him! It said:

To Treasure Hunter Orbit Zwibble
The Zwibble Dibble Mill
Headquarters for Earth Magic
Buzzville Forest
Planet Earth

Dear Orbit,
We are proud to announce the birth of four beautiful emerald slanty birds. Their names are Una, Duna, Tuna, and Buna. Soon we will move into our new home on the rain forest land that you and your family saved with your pennies. Keep up the good work. We still need lots of help here.
Thanks for everything.
The Emerald Slanty Birds